Tea FOR Ruby

by
SARAH FERGUSON
THE DUCHESS OF YORK

illustrated by
ROBIN PREISS GLASSER

SIMON AND SCHUSTER
London New York Sydney

2009
Love Ives
mama
Adelaide

To Beatrice and Eugenie—
you make my world complete
— S F

For Jacqueline Preiss Weitzman—
my sister, my partner, my friend
— R P G

SIMON AND SCHUSTER
First published in Great Britain in 2008 by Simon and Schuster UK Ltd
222 Gray's Inn Road, London WC1X 8HB
A CBS COMPANY

This paperback edition published in 2009
Originally published in 2008 by Simon & Schuster Books for Young Readers,
an imprint of Simon & Schuster Children's Publishing Division, New York

Text copyright © 2008 Sarah Ferguson, The Duchess of York
Illustrations copyright © 2008 Robin Preiss Glasser
All rights reserved.

The rights of Sarah Ferguson and Robin Preiss Glasser to be identified as the author and illustrator of this work
have been asserted by them in accordance with the Copyright, Designs and Patents Act, 1988

All rights reserved including the right of reproduction in whole or in part in any form.

A CIP catalogue record for this book is available from the British Library upon request.

ISBN 978 1 84738 522 2

Printed in China
2 4 6 8 10 9 7 5 3 1

You are invited
to have tea with
The Queen
on Sunday.

Please bring your very best manners.

the Queen."

"I've been invited to have tea with the Queen!"

"Ruby, I hope you won't interrupt when you have tea with . . .

"The Queen."

The Queen.

"I've been invited to have tea with the Queen!"

"Ruby, I hope you will dress appropriately when you have tea with . . .

the Queen.

"I've been invited to have tea with the Queen!"

Only 6 items at a time in dressing rooms, please.

"Ruby, I hope you will say 'please' and 'thank you' when you have tea with . . ."

"The Queen"

oops

"Ruby, I hope you won't talk when you shouldn't when you have tea with ..."

"The Queen."

"I've been invited to have tea with the Queen!"

"Ruby, I hope you will remember to welcome people when you have tea with . . .

The Queen.

"Ruby, I hope you won't talk with your mouth full and won't tip your chair back and will use your fork and napkin when you have tea with ...

The Queen,"

"Tomorrow I'm having tea with the Queen!"

"Ruby, I hope you'll remember to sit up straight when you have tea with the Queen."

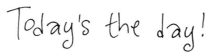

Today's the day!

"Let's hurry
so we won't be late!"

Remember to chew with my mouth closed.

Remember not to speak with my mouth full.

Remember to say "please" and "thank you."

Remember to welcome people.

Remember to use my fork and napkin.

Remember not to interrupt.

Remember not to shout.

Remember to wait my turn.

Remember to sit up straight.

Remember not to talk when I shouldn't.

"GRANDMA?"

"My princess!"

Royal Teatery
Victorian Times
Versailles
Palaces of St. Petersburg
Castles of England

"May I offer you more tea, Princess Ruby?"

"Oh, yes, please, Grandma. Thank you."